ArtScroll Youth Series®

Rabbi Nosson Scherman / Rabbi Meir Zlotowitz

General Editors

Children's Book of Yonah

by Shmuel Blitz
Illustrated by Tova Katz

Introduction by
Rabbi Nosson Scherman

The ArtScroll

Published by

Mesorah Publications, ltd

*The author dedicates this book
to his first grandchild
Dov Meir Blitz*

RTSCROLL YOUTH SERIES®

"ARTSCROLL CHILDREN'S BOOK OF YONAH"

© *Copyright 2006 by* Mesorah Publications, Ltd.
First edition – First impression: August, 2006

Published by **MESORAH PUBLICATIONS, LTD.**
4401 Second Avenue / Brooklyn, N.Y 11232 / (718) 921-9000 / Fax: (718) 680-1875
www.artscroll.com

Distributed in Israel by SIFRIATI / A. GITLER — BOOKS
6 Hayarkon Street / Bnei Brak 51127

Distributed in Europe by LEHMANNS
Unit E, Viking Business Park, Rolling Mill Road / Jarrow, Tyne and Wear / England NE32 3DP

Distributed in Australia and New Zealand by GOLD'S WORLD OF JUDAICA
3-13 William Street / Balaclava, Melbourne 3183, Victoria, Australia

Distributed in South Africa by KOLLEL BOOKSHOP
Ivy Common, 105 William Road / Norwood 2192 / Johannesburg, South Africa

Printed in the USA by Noble Book Press Corp.
Custom bound by Sefercraft, Inc. / 4401 Second Avenue / Brooklyn N.Y. 11232

ISBN: 1-4226-0130-7   (h/c)
      1-4226-0131-5   (p/b)

Introduction
The Book of Yonah and Yom Kippur

It is Minchah time on Yom Kippur. There are only a few hours left to plead with Hashem for a good year. At Minchah, we will read the *Book of Yonah*. Of all the chapters in *Nach* (the Books of the Prophets), the Sages picked the *Book of Yonah*. Why is that story so very, very important for Yom Kippur?

Hashem Is Everywhere

After Shlomo HaMelech died, ten of the twelve tribes made a new kingdom. It was called the Ten Tribes. Most kings of the Ten Tribes were bad people. They served idols and led Jews away from obeying Hashem and the Torah. Hashem sent many prophets to urge the people to repent — to do *teshuvah* — but they did not listen. One of those prophets was Yonah.

Then Hashem gave Yonah an important mission. He sent Yonah to Nineveh, a very big city in Assyria (a country that today is called Iraq). Hashem commanded Yonah to tell the people of Nineveh that their city would be overturned, because they were doing bad things. Yonah did not want to go. He knew that the Jewish people of the Ten Tribes were not repenting. He was afraid that if the people of Nineveh repented, it would seem that they were much better than the Jews.

Yonah loved his people more than he cared about himself. He decided that he would get on a boat and escape from Eretz Yisrael, so he would not have to go to Nineveh. Hashem brought a terrible storm that almost sank the boat. Yonah told the sailors that it was his fault because he did not listen to Hashem. He told the sailors to throw him overboard. They did — and the storm stopped!

Hashem sent a huge fish to swallow Yonah and save him from drowning. Finally, Yonah himself repented and the fish brought him to Nineveh.

Yonah Goes to Nineveh

The people of Nineveh were doing many sins. That is why Yonah told them that Hashem would "overturn" the city. The word "overturn" can mean two things. If you pick up something, turn it upside down and throw it to the ground, you will break it. If that is what Hashem would do to Nineveh, the city would be destroyed and many people would die. But overturn can also mean something else. It can mean that the city and its people would change so much that they would be altogether different. If the people stopped doing bad things and began acting the way Hashem wanted them to, it would be as if they had turned themselves upside down.

When the king and people of Nineveh heard what Yonah said, they became very frightened. What would happen to them? Would they all die?

They did two things. First they started fasting and wearing clothes that showed how sad they were. But that was not the main thing Hashem wanted.

Then the people of Nineveh did something else. They started being nice to one another. They gave back things that they had stolen. They stopped being mean. That is what Hashem wanted. It meant that the people of Nineveh were really changing and repenting.

The city of Nineveh was being overturned, because its people were repenting! It did not have to be destroyed anymore!

That is why we read the *Book of Yonah* on Yom Kippur. It teaches us that it is not possible to run away from Hashem. King David already said in *Tehillim* (Psalm 139) that wherever someone tries to go, Hashem is there. We cannot escape from him. Why should we even want to? The greatest honor anyone could ever have is to serve Hashem!

The *Book of Yonah* also reminds us that it is never too late to repent. Hashem does not want to punish us. He wants to be kind and generous to us, and He wants us to deserve it.

Let us read about Yonah in this beautiful book by Shmuel Blitz. He explains the *Book of Yonah* according to the teachings of our Sages. The illustrations of Tova Katz make us feel as if we are there watching everything as it happens.

The best thing about this book is that it will help us understand what we can do to make Yom Kippur a day when Hashem will forgive our sins and bless us, our families, and all of *Klal Yisrael* with a very good year.

Rabbi Nosson Scherman

Table of Contents

Chapter 1   8

Hashem tells Yonah, a prophet, to travel to Nineveh, a non-Jewish city. There he should tell the people that they have acted badly and their city will be overturned. Yonah tries to run away by taking a ship to Tarshish, but a strong storm almost sinks the ship. The sailors are sure that Hashem sent the storm to punish someone. They throw lots to find out who it is. The lots show that the storm is because of Yonah. The sailors throw him overboard, and the storm stops.

Chapter 2   22

Hashem sends a large fish to swallow Yonah. While inside the fish, Yonah repents and decides to obey Hashem and go to Nineveh. He prays to Hashem to save him. The fish spits Yonah out back onto dry land.

Chapter 3   32

Hashem once again tells Yonah to go to Nineveh. This time Yonah goes and announces that the city will be overturned. The people of Nineveh listen to Yonah and believe him. Everyone in the city, even the king, fasts and prays. They also stop doing bad things. Hashem sees that they repented and He does not destroy the city.

Chapter 4   40

Yonah is unhappy that Hashem did not overturn Nineveh. Yonah wants to die. He makes a hut for himself and Hashem makes a big plant grow to give him shade. Yonah feels much better. Hashem then sends a worm to kill the plant. Yonah feels bad again and asks to die. Hashem shows Yonah that if a simple plant is so important to him, shouldn't a big city full of people be much more important?

A Note About the Translation:

The English that appears alongside the Hebrew text is designed for children, and is a simplified adaptation rather than a literal translation.

¹ **A**nd the word of Hashem came to Yonah the son of Amittai, saying:

א וַיְהִי דְּבַר־יהוה אֶל־יוֹנָה בֶן־אֲמִתַּי לֵאמְר:

Did You Know??

Who was Yonah?

One day, the prophet Eliyahu visited a very poor woman in in the village of Tzarfas. She and her son had no money and almost nothing to eat. They were starving to death. Eliyahu came and blessed her. A miracle happened and Hashem gave her much food.

Soon after this incident, the young boy died. The woman called for Eliyahu, who came and brought the young boy back to life. This boy was Yonah. (This story appears in *Sefer Melachim*, the Book of I Kings, 17:10 24.)

When Yonah grew up, he became a student of Eliyahu. After Eliyahu went up to heaven, Yonah became a student of the prophet Elisha. Elisha had been Eliyahu's greatest student, and then became Eliyahu's successor.

A Closer Look

Yonah was attending the *Simchas Beis HaShoeivah*, the Water Pouring Ceremony in the *Beis HaMikdash* in Yerushalayim, when he received this prophecy. It was his first prophecy from Hashem.

²"Get up! Go to Nineveh, the great city, and cry out against it, because their wickedness has come up before Me."

ב קוּם לֵךְ אֶל־נִינְוֵה הָעִיר הַגְּדוֹלָה וּקְרָא עָלֶיהָ כִּי־עָלְתָה רָעָתָם לְפָנָי:

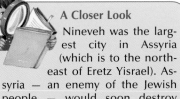

A Closer Look
Nineveh was the largest city in Assyria (which is to the northeast of Eretz Yisrael). Assyria — an enemy of the Jewish people — would soon destroy the Ten Tribes of Israel and scatter them throughout the world.

Did You Know??
The great warrior, Nimrod, was the original builder of the city of Nineveh, nearly a thousand years earlier. He was the evil king who threw Avraham Avinu into the fiery furnace.

9

³ Yonah got up and fled to Tarshish, as if to get away from Hashem. He went to Yaffo, and found a boat there going to Tarshish. He paid the fare and went onto the boat to go with them to Tarshish running away from Hashem.

ג וַיָּ֣קׇם יוֹנָ֗ה לִבְרֹ֤חַ תַּרְשִׁ֙ישָׁה֙ מִלִּפְנֵ֣י יְהֹוָ֔ה וַיֵּ֨רֶד יָפ֜וֹ וַיִּמְצָ֥א אֳנִיָּ֣ה ׀ בָּאָ֣ה תַרְשִׁ֗ישׁ וַיִּתֵּ֨ן שְׂכָרָ֜הּ וַיֵּ֤רֶד בָּהּ֙ לָב֤וֹא עִמָּהֶם֙ תַּרְשִׁ֔ישָׁה מִלִּפְנֵ֖י יְהֹוָֽה:

Did You Know??
There are different opinions about exactly where Tarshish was. Some say it was in Spain, some say it was in Tunisia, and some say it was in Southern Turkey. But everyone agrees that it was outside Eretz Yisrael, and in the opposite direction from Nineveh.

A Closer Look
Why did Yonah not listen to Hashem? Why did he run away from doing what Hashem had commanded him to do?
Yonah was afraid that the people of Nineveh would repent and be forgiven by Hashem. Then Hashem would be very angry with the Jewish people because they did not repent. If that happened, Yonah was afraid the people of Nineveh would be able to destroy the Jewish people (as they nearly did when they, indeed, later conquered the Ten Tribes).
Even if he would get punished, Yonah did not want to be part of causing the destruction of the Jewish people.
Yonah assumed that if he left Eretz Yisrael, Hashem would no longer give him such missions.

Did You Know??
Yonah was in such a rush for the boat to leave that he bought all the unsold places on the ship so that it could set sail immediately.

⁴ Then Hashem caused a mighty wind to blow on the sea. It became such a huge storm on the sea that it seemed as if the boat would be destroyed.

ד וַיהוָה הֵטִיל רֽוּחַ־גְּדוֹלָה אֶל־הַיָּם וַיְהִי סַֽעַר־גָּדוֹל בַּיָּם וְהָאֳנִיָּה חִשְּׁבָה לְהִשָּׁבֵֽר:

⁵ The sailors became frightened. Each one cried out to his own god. They all tossed their possessions overboard to lighten the load on the ship. Yonah had gone down inside the ship. He lay down, and fell asleep.

ה וַיִּירְא֣וּ הַמַּלָּחִ֗ים וַיִּזְעֲקוּ֮ אִ֣ישׁ אֶל־אֱלֹהָיו֒ וַיָּטִ֜לוּ אֶת־הַכֵּלִ֣ים אֲשֶׁ֣ר בָּאֳנִיָּ֗ה אֶל־הַיָּם֙ לְהָקֵ֣ל מֵֽעֲלֵיהֶ֔ם וְיוֹנָ֗ה יָרַד֙ אֶל־יַרְכְּתֵ֣י הַסְּפִינָ֔ה וַיִּשְׁכַּ֖ב וַיֵּרָדַֽם׃

A Closer Look

Each prayed to his own god. Everyone decided that the god that saves them would be accepted as the true god. But obviously, none of their false gods were able to save them.

Did You Know??

All the experienced sailors were frightened because they had never seen such a strong storm. They were sure the boat would sink and they would all drown.

A Closer Look

Our Rabbis teach us that while all the sailors were praying, Yonah went to sleep and did not pray. Since he had just run away from doing what Hashem had commanded him to do, he did not think that Hashem would answer his prayers.

⁶ The captain of the ship came to Yonah and said to him, "How can you sleep? Get up and call to your God. Maybe your God will reconsider our fate and we will not die."

וַיִּקְרַב אֵלָיו רַב הַחֹבֵל וַיֹּאמֶר לוֹ מַה־לְּךָ נִרְדָּם קוּם קְרָא אֶל־אֱלֹהֶיךָ אוּלַי יִתְעַשֵּׁת הָאֱלֹהִים לָנוּ וְלֹא נֹאבֵד:

Did You Know??
Since Yonah had paid the full cost of the boat so that it would leave immediately, there were not many passengers. That is why the captain immediately noticed that Yonah was missing, and was not praying to his God, like everyone else.

13

⁷ Then each person said to the other, "Let us cast lots, so we can decide who is responsible for this horrible disaster that is happening to us." They cast lots, and the lot fell on Yonah.

ז וַיֹּאמְר֞וּ אִ֣ישׁ אֶל־רֵעֵ֗הוּ לְכוּ֙ וְנַפִּ֣ילָה גֽוֹרָל֔וֹת וְנֵ֣דְעָ֔ה בְּשֶׁלְּמִ֛י הָרָעָ֥ה הַזֹּ֖את לָ֑נוּ וַיַּפִּ֙לוּ֙ גּֽוֹרָל֔וֹת וַיִּפֹּ֥ל הַגּוֹרָ֖ל עַל־יוֹנָֽה:

A Closer Look
The crew saw that other ships where sailing peacefully nearby. Only their ship was caught in this horrible storm. They therefore knew that they were in danger because of someone on their ship. They decided to cast lots to see who the guilty one was.

Did You Know??
They didn't cast lots just once. They did it a few times, to make sure that they would find the true guilty party. The lot fell on Yonah every time.

14

⁸ They said to him, "Tell us now. Who made this terrible thing happen to us? What kind of work do you do? Where do you come from? What is your country? And who are your people?"

ח וַיֹּאמְרוּ אֵלָיו הַגִּידָה־נָּא לָנוּ בַּאֲשֶׁר לְמִי־הָרָעָה הַזֹּאת לָנוּ מַה־מְּלַאכְתְּךָ וּמֵאַיִן תָּבוֹא מָה אַרְצֶךָ וְאֵי־מִזֶּה עַם אָתָּה:

A Closer Look

They asked Yonah all these questions to try to understand why this terrible thing was happening to the ship, and why he was being punished. Each of these questions hinted at a different reason he might be being punished.

Who has caused this calamity? Maybe you owe someone money or maybe you have insulted someone.

What kind of work do you do? Maybe you are doing dishonest work.

Where do you come from? Maybe you come from a cursed city.

What is your country? Who are your people? Maybe you come from a sinful place.

15

⁹ He said to them, "I am a Hebrew. I fear Hashem, the God of the Heavens, Who had made the sea and the dry land."

ט וַיֹּאמֶר אֲלֵיהֶם עִבְרִי אָנֹכִי וְאֶת־יהוָה אֱלֹהֵי הַשָּׁמַיִם אֲנִי יָרֵא אֲשֶׁר־עָשָׂה אֶת־הַיָּם וְאֶת־הַיַּבָּשָׁה:

Did You Know??
Until the exile of the Ten Tribes from Israel the Jewish people were often referred to as Hebrews. After that, they were usually referred to as Jews.

A Closer Look
Since Hashem created the sea and the dry land, He can stop the storm whenever He wishes.

A Closer Look
Yonah's statement that he is a Jew who fears Hashem is the answer to all of the sailors' questions. Since he fears Hashem, he does only honest work. His people, the Jewish people, are honest in all their dealings.

¹⁰ The men became very frightened and they asked him, "What have you done?" They knew that he was running way from Hashem because He had told them.

י וַיִּירְאוּ הָאֲנָשִׁים יִרְאָה גְדוֹלָה וַיֹּאמְרוּ אֵלָיו מַה־זֹּאת עָשִׂיתָ כִּי־יָדְעוּ הָאֲנָשִׁים כִּי־מִלִּפְנֵי יהוה הוּא בֹרֵחַ כִּי הִגִּיד לָהֶם:

A Closer Look
They could not understand how Yonah thought he would be able to run away from Hashem, no matter where he went. They understood that Hashem is the God of the whole world, and that Yonah could not hide from Him, anywhere.

¹¹ They said to him, "What should we do to you to make the sea become calm, because the sea is getting stormier?"

יא וַיֹּאמְרוּ אֵלָיו מַה־נַּעֲשֶׂה לָּךְ וְיִשְׁתֹּק הַיָּם מֵעָלֵינוּ כִּי הַיָּם הוֹלֵךְ וְסֹעֵר:

A Closer Look

Since the sailors now understood that Yonah was a prophet of Hashem, they did not want to harm him, and they looked to him for an answer to their problem. They thought that if they brought Yonah back to the shores of Eretz Yisrael, the problem might be solved.

¹² He said to them, "Pick me up and throw me into the sea. Then the sea will calm down. I know that it is because of me that this giant storm is upon you."

יב וַיֹּאמֶר אֲלֵיהֶם שָׂאוּנִי וַהֲטִילֻנִי אֶל־הַיָּם וְיִשְׁתֹּק הַיָּם מֵעֲלֵיכֶם כִּי יוֹדֵעַ אָנִי כִּי בְשֶׁלִּי הַסַּעַר הַגָּדוֹל הַזֶּה עֲלֵיכֶם:

Did You Know??

Yonah did not want the sailors to bring him back to Eretz Yisrael. He preferred death to possibly having a role in the enemies of the Jews bringing destruction upon the Jewish people. He also reassured the sailors that no harm would come to them for throwing him into the sea, as the entire storm was because of his sin.

17

יג וַיַּחְתְּרוּ הָאֲנָשִׁים לְהָשִׁיב אֶל־הַיַּבָּשָׁה וְלֹא יָכֹלוּ כִּי הַיָּם הוֹלֵךְ וְסֹעֵר עֲלֵיהֶם:

[13] Still, the sailors tried rowing with all their might to bring the ship back to the shore. But they could not succeed, because the sea just kept growing stormier.

A Closer Look

The sailors did not want to harm Yonah, a prophet of Hashem, even though he told them to throw him overboard.

¹⁴ They all cried out to Hashem and said, "Please, Hashem, let us not be destroyed because of this man. And do not blame us for shedding innocent blood. You, Hashem, have done just as You wanted."

יד וַיִּקְרְאוּ אֶל־יהוה וַיֹּאמְרוּ אָנָּה יהוה אַל־נָא נֹאבְדָה בְּנֶפֶשׁ הָאִישׁ הַזֶּה וְאַל־תִּתֵּן עָלֵינוּ דָּם נָקִיא כִּי־אַתָּה יהוה כַּאֲשֶׁר חָפַצְתָּ עָשִׂיתָ:

Did You Know??

At the beginning, all the sailors prayed to their own gods. By now they all believed fully in Hashem. They understood that their gods were useless.

A Closer Look

The sailors were saying that they were being Hashem's messengers to throw Yonah into the sea. Therefore, they asked, "Please do not hold us responsible for murdering him."

19

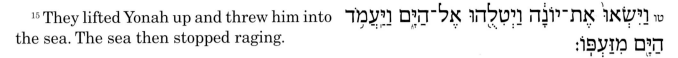

¹⁵ They lifted Yonah up and threw him into the sea. The sea then stopped raging.

טו וַיִּשְׂאוּ אֶת־יוֹנָה וַיְטִלֻהוּ אֶל־הַיָּם וַיַּעֲמֹד הַיָּם מִזַּעְפּוֹ:

Did You Know??

The sailors threw Yonah into the sea little by little. First they lifted him up and put him into the sea up to his knees. The storm quieted. When they lifted him out of the water, the storm started to rage again. Then, they put him into the sea up to his stomach. Again the sea quieted, but when they lifted him up, it again began to rage. Finally they put him in up to his neck. When the exact same thing happened, they realized they had no choice and threw him completely into the sea.

16 The men were all in awe of Hashem. They offered a sacrifice to Hashem and made vows.

טז וַיִּירְאוּ הָאֲנָשִׁים יִרְאָה גְדוֹלָה אֶת־יְהֹוָה וַיִּזְבְּחוּ־זֶבַח לַיהֹוָה וַיִּדְּרוּ נְדָרִים:

A Closer Look

This means they vowed to bring sacrifices to the *Beis HaMikdash*, and to give charity to the poor. Some of our Sages say that they even vowed to convert to Judaism after seeing the awesome power of Hashem!

א וַיְמַן יְהוָה דָּג גָּדוֹל לִבְלֹעַ אֶת־יוֹנָה וַיְהִי יוֹנָה בִּמְעֵי הַדָּג שְׁלֹשָׁה יָמִים וּשְׁלֹשָׁה לֵילוֹת:

[1] And Hashem then sent a large fish to swallow Yonah; Yonah remained in the fish's belly for three days and three nights.

Did You Know??
Hashem prepared this fish during the six days of Creation. The fish waited around all those years for the exact moment when it would swallow Yonah, so that he would not drown.

A Closer Look
A person cannot stay alive in a fish's belly for more than a few minutes, because there is no oxygen to breathe! It was a miracle that Yonah stayed alive for three days and three nights.

Did You Know??
People usually think of this big fish as being a whale. But the *pasuk* does not tell us that; it says only that it was a big fish. Exactly what kind of fish it was is not important.

² Yonah prayed to Hashem, his God, from the belly of the fish.

ב וַיִּתְפַּלֵּל יוֹנָה אֶל־יהוה אֱלֹהָיו מִמְּעֵי הַדָּגָה:

A Closer Look
The rest of this chapter tells us Yonah's prayer to Hashem.

³ And he said, "I called out in my trouble to Hashem, and He answered me. I cried out from the belly of a world below, and You heard my prayer.

ג וַיֹּאמֶר קָרָאתִי מִצָּרָה לִי אֶל־יהוה וַיַּעֲנֵנִי מִבֶּטֶן שְׁאוֹל שִׁוַּעְתִּי שָׁמַעְתָּ קוֹלִי:

A Closer Look
Hashem wanted Yonah to realize that he had sinned, and that he must pray to Him.

24

A Closer Look

It would seem from the wording of this prayer that Yonah said this prayer *after* being saved. But most of our Sages say that Yonah said this prayer while still in the belly of the fish. He was sure that Hashem would listen to his prayer and save him; so he recited this prayer as if he had already been saved.

Yonah knew that if Hashem had wanted him to die, he would not have stayed alive inside the fish. Therefore, Hashem must have wanted him to live – and pray and repent.

If we see that Hashem is helping or saving us, it is a sign that He wants us to do *teshuvah*; We must make sure that we deserve His help.

A Closer Look

It would seem that Yonah did not deserve to be saved by Hashem, because he had run away, but Hashem saved him anyway. We see how truly merciful Hashem is.

⁴ "You threw me into the depths, into the heart of the seas. The waters swirled around me, the waves swept over me.

ד וַתַּשְׁלִיכֵנִי מְצוּלָה בִּלְבַב יַמִּים וְנָהָר יְסֹבְבֵנִי כָּל־מִשְׁבָּרֶיךָ וְגַלֶּיךָ עָלַי עָבָרוּ:

A Closer Look
Even though it was the sailors who took Yonah and threw him into the sea, Yonah understood that it was really Hashem Who made it happen. The sailors were only Hashem's messengers.

26

⁵ "And I thought, 'I may have been removed from Your sight; but instead, one day, I will look upon Your Holy Temple once again.'

ה וַאֲנִי אָמַרְתִּי נִגְרַשְׁתִּי מִנֶּגֶד עֵינֶיךָ אַךְ אוֹסִיף לְהַבִּיט אֶל־הֵיכַל קָדְשֶׁךָ:

A Closer Look

This is what Yonah was thinking as he was being thrown overboard into the sea. He was afraid that since he had run away from Eretz Yisrael, he would never be allowed to return. But when he saw that Hashem made a miracle to save him, he knew that he would one day return to Eretz Yisrael and see the Holy Temple again.

27

6 "Water totally surrounded me, until I almost died. The ocean deep spun around me, and weeds were tangled around my head.

וַ אֲפָפֿוּנִי מַיִם עַד־נֶ֫פֶשׁ תְּהוֹם יְסֹבְבֵ֫נִי סוּף חָבוּשׁ לְרֹאשִׁי:

A Closer Look
All this was happening to Yonah before the giant fish came and swallowed him up.

7 "I sank down to the foot of the mountains that are in the sea. I was sure that the earth was locked to me, not letting me return there. But You lifted me from the pit, Hashem, my God.

ז לְקִצְבֵ֣י הָרִים֮ יָרַ֗דְתִּי הָאָ֛רֶץ בְּרִחֶ֥יהָ בַעֲדִ֖י לְעוֹלָ֑ם וַתַּ֧עַל מִשַּׁ֛חַת חַיַּ֖י יְהֹוָ֥ה אֱלֹהָֽי:

A Closer Look
Yonah was sinking further and further down, reaching the bottom of the ocean floor. He was rescued just when he was about to die. Our Sages teach us that we should never lose faith in Hashem. He can save us in the wink of an eye, even if a sword is already on our neck. Nothing is too hard for Hashem.

⁸ "My spirit was weak, but I remembered Hashem. My prayer came to You, up to the Heavens.

ח בְּהִתְעַטֵּף עָלַי נַפְשִׁי אֶת־יְהֹוָה זָכָרְתִּי וַתָּבוֹא אֵלֶיךָ תְּפִלָּתִי אֶל הֵיכַל קָדְשֶׁךָ:

A Closer Look
Even with all this going on around him, Yonah remembered that the only thing for him to do was to pray to Hashem.

⁹ "The other nations value things that are worthless, and abandon receiving kindness from You.

ט מְשַׁמְּרִים הַבְלֵי־שָׁוְא חַסְדָּם יַעֲזֹבוּ:

Did You Know??
As long as the nations worship idols, they will never understand or receive Hashem's true kindness.

29

10 "But I thank You and will bring an offering to You. Everything that I promised, I will do, for Hashem has saved me."

יוַאֲנִי בְּקוֹל תּוֹדָה אֶזְבְּחָה־לָּךְ אֲשֶׁר נָדַרְתִּי אֲשַׁלֵּמָה יְשׁוּעָתָה לַיהוָה:

Did You Know??

Four types of people need to give special thanks to Hashem for being saved: Someone who traveled across the sea, someone who traveled across a wilderness, someone who has recovered from an illness, and someone who has been let out of prison. In the time of the *Beis Hamikdash*, such people brought a special *korban* of thanksgiving. It was called a *Korban Todah*. Nowadays, such people make a special *berachah* (Blessed are You, Hashem, our God, King of the Universe, ... Who has granted me wonderful favors) to thank Hashem for saving them.

¹¹ Hashem then instructed the fish, and it spat Yonah out onto dry land.

יא וַיֹּאמֶר יהוה לַדָּג וַיָּקֵא אֶת־יוֹנָה אֶל־הַיַּבָּשָׁה:

A Closer Look
Hashem listened to Yonah and accepted his prayers and his repentence.

Did You Know??
After being in the belly of the fish for three days and three nights, Yonah was spat out with his clothing in tatters, his hair fallen out, and his skin all shriveled.

A Closer Look
The *pasuk* does not tell us whether the fish spat Yonah out in Eretz Yisrael or in a place closer to Nineveh, so he would be able to continue on his mission.

31

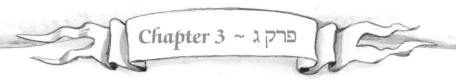

1 And the Word of Hashem came to Yonah a second time, saying:

א וַיְהִי דְבַר־יְהוָה אֶל־יוֹנָה שֵׁנִית לֵאמֹר:

A Closer Look
When Hashem first sent Yonah to Nineveh he did not obey. Now he repented and was sorry for not listening, so Hashem gave him a second chance. The best way for someone to prove that he is sorry for doing wrong is to get another chance, and then to do the right thing.

2 "Get up! Go to Nineveh, the great city, and call out to them the prophecy that I will tell you."

ב קוּם לֵךְ אֶל־נִינְוֵה הָעִיר הַגְּדוֹלָה וּקְרָא אֵלֶיהָ אֶת־הַקְּרִיאָה אֲשֶׁר אָנֹכִי דֹּבֵר אֵלֶיךָ:

Did You Know??
Hashem told Yonah to tell the people what they did wrong. Yonah was supposed to tell them that if they do not repent, their great city would be destroyed in another forty days.

³ Yonah got up and went to Nineveh, just as Hashem had told him to do. Nineveh was a very large city. It was a three-day walk.

ג וַיָּ֤קָם יוֹנָה֙ וַיֵּ֣לֶךְ אֶל־נִֽינְוֶ֔ה כִּדְבַ֖ר יְהֹוָ֑ה וְנִֽינְוֵ֗ה הָיְתָ֤ה עִיר־גְּדוֹלָה֙ לֵֽאלֹהִ֔ים מַהֲלַ֖ךְ שְׁלֹ֥שֶׁת יָמִֽים:

Did You Know??
This means that the city of Nineveh was so big that it took three days to walk across it. Because it was so big, people could not imagine it being destroyed.

⁴ Yonah began to enter the city and walked for one full day. He called out and said, "In forty more days, Nineveh will be overturned!"

ד וַיָּחֶל יוֹנָה לָבוֹא בָעִיר מַהֲלַךְ יוֹם אֶחָד וַיִּקְרָא וַיֹּאמַר עוֹד אַרְבָּעִים יוֹם וְנִינְוֵה נֶהְפָּכֶת:

A Closer Look

Yonah announced that Nineveh would be destroyed in forty days. But the people repented, and Hashem did not destroy the city. This shows that if a person repents, Hashem will change a bad decree.

Hashem used the word נֶהְפָּכֶת, which really means "overturned," not destroyed. The word "overturned" can mean two different things. It can mean "turned upside down" and destroyed. Or it can mean completely changed. When the people of Nineveh repented, the city did turn over, because it changed. It did not have to be destroyed.

Did You Know??

After walking for an entire day, Yonah was near the middle of Nineveh. He then warned the people, telling them that they must repent.

34

⁵ The people of Nineveh believed in Hashem, so they ordered everyone to fast and wear sackcloth — everyone in the city, both big and small.

ה וַיַּאֲמִינוּ אַנְשֵׁי נִינְוֵה בֵּאלֹהִים וַיִּקְרְאוּ־צוֹם וַיִּלְבְּשׁוּ שַׂקִּים מִגְּדוֹלָם וְעַד־קְטַנָּם:

Did You Know??
By a miracle, Yonah's voice was heard by everyone in the city. When they heard his voice, and what he had to say, everyone decided to repent.

A Closer Look
In Shushan, during the time of the Purim story, Queen Esther called for a fast to bring the people to repent.

A Closer Look
Why were the people of Nineveh so ready to repent? Because the sailors who were on the ship with Yonah told the people how they had thrown him into the sea and about how he had been miraculously rescued. When the people heard this, they believed that Yonah was a holy man, a messenger of God, and the people became afraid of Hashem.

⁶ When news of this reached the king of Nineveh, he got up from his throne, removed his royal robe, put on a sackcloth, and sat down on ashes.

וּ וַיִּגַּע הַדָּבָר אֶל־מֶלֶךְ נִינְוֵה וַיָּקָם מִכִּסְאוֹ וַיַּעֲבֵר אַדַּרְתּוֹ מֵעָלָיו וַיְכַס שַׂק וַיֵּשֶׁב עַל־הָאֵפֶר:

Did You Know??
It is not clear who the king was. Some Sages say he was Osnapper who is mentioned in other places in *Tanach*. *Pirkei d'Rabbi Eliezer* says that the king was Pharaoh of Egypt, the same Pharaoh who had survived Hashem's punishment at the Sea of Reeds when the Jewish people left Egypt.

A Closer Look
By doing all these things, the king of Nineveh humbled himself and made it clear to everyone that he believed in Hashem.

⁷ And he gave orders and commanded all of Nineveh, "From the office of the king and his nobles, let it be known: Man and animal, cows and sheep, no one shall taste anything, nor graze from the ground, nor drink any water.

ז וַיַּזְעֵק וַיֹּאמֶר בְּנִינְוֵה מִטַּעַם הַמֶּלֶךְ וּגְדֹלָיו לֵאמֹר הָאָדָם וְהַבְּהֵמָה הַבָּקָר וְהַצֹּאן אַל־יִטְעֲמוּ מְאוּמָה אַל־יִרְעוּ וּמַיִם אַל־יִשְׁתּוּ:

Did You Know??
The king commanded the people not to feed their animals. This made them even sadder, and more likely to repent.

A Closer Look
People had been very affected by Yonah's words. And now their king commanded them to repent. It is not surprising that everyone repented!

⁸ "Everyone should be dressed in sackcloth — both man and beast, and everyone should cry out and pray to God. From today on, everyone should stop their evil ways, and stop stealing.

ח וְיִתְכַּסּוּ שַׂקִּים הָאָדָם וְהַבְּהֵמָה וְיִקְרְאוּ אֶל־אֱלֹהִים בְּחׇזְקָה וְיָשֻׁבוּ אִישׁ מִדַּרְכּוֹ הָרָעָה וּמִן־הֶחָמָס אֲשֶׁר בְּכַפֵּיהֶם:

Did You Know??

When the king ordered the animals to be dressed in sackcloth, he was talking about his royal horses. He did not order everyone to put sackcloth on the animals in the field.

A Closer Look

It would not be enough if the people would just fast and pray. To really repent, the people would actually stop doing bad things.

A Closer Look

How did the people pray? They held up their infants and asked God to have mercy on them and on their other children who had not yet sinned.

⁹ "Whoever knows that he sinned, let him repent, and God will not punish him. God will turn away from His burning anger, and we will not be destroyed."

ט מִי־יוֹדֵעַ יָשׁוּב וְנִחַם הָאֱלֹהִים וְשָׁב מֵחֲרוֹן אַפּוֹ וְלֹא נֹאבֵד:

Did You Know??

Hashem does not change His mind. Only people change their minds. This verse means that when someone repents, he becomes like a new person who does not deserve to be punished.

A Closer Look

The king told the people that even if they sinned in private, and no one knew about it, they still must repent — because Hashem knows what they did.

A Closer Look

The king said that Hashem sent Yonah the prophet to warn them, because He wanted to give the people of Nineveh another chance. If He wanted only to destroy the city and did not want to give them another chance to repent, He would not have sent the prophet to them.

¹⁰ And God saw what the people had done, and how they had repented from their evil ways, and He did not do the bad thing He said He would do to them.

י וַיַּרְא הָאֱלֹהִים אֶת־מַעֲשֵׂיהֶם כִּי־שָׁבוּ מִדַּרְכָּם הָרָעָה וַיִּנָּחֶם הָאֱלֹהִים עַל־הָרָעָה אֲשֶׁר־דִּבֶּר לַעֲשׂוֹת־לָהֶם וְלֹא עָשָׂה:

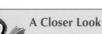

A Closer Look

The *pasuk* shows us that it was not important to Hashem that the people fasted or wore sackcloth. What mattered to Him was seeing that they stopped doing bad things and repented. There are three parts to repenting: admitting that you did something wrong, feeling bad about it, and making sure never to do it again. If we hurt someone, we must also ask that person to forgive us and return what we took or pay what we owe.

Did You Know??

Hashem gave the people forty days to repent. Our Sages tell us that later on the people of Nineveh went back to their evil ways. Forty years later (reminding us of the forty days they had to repent), Hashem destroyed the city of Nineveh.

A Closer Look

We see that an evil decree can be changed if a person is sorry for what he did and then starts doing the right thing.

¹ Yonah felt very bad about all this, and it bothered him.

א וַיֵּרַע אֶל־יוֹנָה רָעָה גְדוֹלָה וַיִּחַר לוֹ:

Did You Know??
What caused Yonah the most pain? The feeling that the Jewish people would not repent. And worse, Nineveh, the city that did listen and repent, was the capital city of the Assyrians, the country that would one day destroy the Ten Tribes of Israel.

A Closer Look
Yonah was sure that the Jews would not listen to a prophet telling them to repent, the way the people of Nineveh had listened. Because of that, the Jewish people would be punished.

Yonah felt that he was being a tool to make his people suffer. This made him very sad. This was why he tried to run away from doing Hashem's command in the first place.

² And he prayed to Hashem, and he said, "Please, Hashem, isn't this exactly what I said would happen when I was still at home? That is why I ran away to Tarshish — because I knew that you are a compassionate God, slow to anger, full of kindness, and relenting from doing harm.

³ "And now, please, Hashem, take my life from me, because I would rather die than live."

ב וַיִּתְפַּלֵּל אֶל־יהוה וַיֹּאמַר אָנָּה יהוה הֲלוֹא־זֶה דְבָרִי עַד־הֱיוֹתִי עַל־אַדְמָתִי עַל־ כֵּן קִדַּמְתִּי לִבְרֹחַ תַּרְשִׁישָׁה כִּי יָדַעְתִּי כִּי אַתָּה אֵל־חַנּוּן וְרַחוּם אֶרֶךְ אַפַּיִם וְרַב־ חֶסֶד וְנִחָם עַל־הָרָעָה: ג וְעַתָּה יהוה קַח־ נָא אֶת־נַפְשִׁי מִמֶּנִּי כִּי טוֹב מוֹתִי מֵחַיָּי:

A Closer Look
Yonah was saying that he would rather die than see the destruction of the Jewish people. This shows how much Yonah loved the nation of Israel.

⁴ And Hashem said, "Are you so deeply upset?"

ד וַיֹּאמֶר יְהֹוָה הַהֵיטֵב חָרָה לָךְ:

A Closer Look

Clearly, Hashem knew how upset Yonah was. He was asking the question only because He wanted to do something that would show Yonah he was wrong. Yonah should not feel bad about Hashem's kindness and mercy for the people of Nineveh.

Hashem was also reminding Yonah that people can always repent. It is wrong to give up hope on anyone, no matter how much they have sinned. Hashem will accept everyone's *teshuvah*.

⁵ Yonah left the city, and stayed in a place east of the city. He made himself a hut there, and sat there in its shade, waiting to see what would happen to the city.

ה וַיֵּצֵא יוֹנָה מִן־הָעִיר וַיֵּשֶׁב מִקֶּדֶם לָעִיר וַיַּעַשׂ לוֹ שָׁם סֻכָּה וַיֵּשֶׁב תַּחְתֶּיהָ בַּצֵּל עַד אֲשֶׁר יִרְאֶה מַה־יִּהְיֶה בָּעִיר:

A Closer Look

The people of Nineveh were given forty days to repent. Yonah planned to stay in the hut for forty days to see what would happen to the city. Even though the people repented, he felt it was possible that they would go back to their old evil ways before the end of the forty days.

A Closer Look

Yonah built himself a small hut to have shade from the hot sun. This hut that Yonah built would be used to teach a very deep lesson.

⁶ Then Hashem provided Yonah with a *kikayon* plant, which grew above Yonah and gave him much shade over his head, to save him from being uncomfortable. Yonah was very happy with the *kikayon* plant.

וַיְמַ֣ן יְהֹוָֽה־אֱ֠לֹהִים קִיקָי֞וֹן וַיַּ֣עַל ׀ מֵעַ֣ל לְיוֹנָ֗ה לִהְי֥וֹת צֵל֙ עַל־רֹאשׁ֔וֹ לְהַצִּ֥יל ל֖וֹ מֵרָֽעָת֑וֹ וַיִּשְׂמַ֥ח יוֹנָ֛ה עַל־הַקִּֽיקָי֖וֹן שִׂמְחָ֥ה גְדוֹלָֽה:

Did You Know??
A *kikayon* is a plant with many big leaves that provide much shade.

A Closer Look
The plant grew miraculously. In one night, it grew to its full size.

A Closer Look
Yonah was very happy because this *kikayon* was a miracle from Hashem. It made him feel that Hashem had forgiven him from trying to run away.

In Nineveh the sun was very strong, and it made Yonah very uncomfortable. The covering of his hut had dried up already, and was not giving him enough shade.

⁷ Then God prepared a worm to appear at daybreak the next morning and attack the *kikayon* plant, and the *kikayon* plant then dried up.

ז וַיְמַן הָאֱלֹהִים תּוֹלַעַת בַּעֲלוֹת הַשַּׁחַר לַמָּחֳרָת וַתַּךְ אֶת־הַקִּיקָיוֹן וַיִּיבָשׁ:

Did You Know??

Yonah was able to enjoy the shade of the *kikayon* for just one day. Then the worm ate its roots until it dried up and the leaves did not give shade anymore.

The *kikayon* plant was destroyed just as the sun was rising. This was when Yonah needed it the most.

⁸ When the sun rose that morning God prepared an unusually strong east wind. The sun beat down on Yonah's head, and he felt faint. He asked for death, saying, "My death would be better than to continue living!"

ח וַיְהִי ׀ כִּזְרֹחַ הַשֶּׁמֶשׁ וַיְמַן אֱלֹהִים רוּחַ קָדִים חֲרִישִׁית וַתַּךְ הַשֶּׁמֶשׁ עַל־רֹאשׁ יוֹנָה וַיִּתְעַלָּף וַיִּשְׁאַל אֶת־נַפְשׁוֹ לָמוּת וַיֹּאמֶר טוֹב מוֹתִי מֵחַיָּי:

Did You Know??
The east wind that blows in Assyria is a strong, uncomfortable, hot wind. The east wind is the strongest of all winds. It is the wind Hashem used to blow back the Sea of Reeds when the Jews left Egypt. It is also the wind that Hashem uses to punish people.

A Closer Look
This wind comes from the east. Yonah had gone to the east of the city, therefore, there was nothing between him and the east wind blowing at him. Yonah was in such pain that he asked Hashem to let him die.

⁹ And God said to Yonah, "Are you so upset because of what happened to the *kikayon* plant?" He anwered, "I am so upset that I wish to die."

ט וַיֹּ֨אמֶר אֱלֹהִים֙ אֶל־יוֹנָ֔ה הַהֵיטֵ֥ב חָרָה־לְךָ֖ עַל־הַקִּֽיקָי֑וֹן וַיֹּ֕אמֶר הֵיטֵ֥ב חָֽרָה־לִ֖י עַד־מָֽוֶת:

> **Did You Know??**
> Hashem did all this to teach Yonah a lesson, as we shall see in the next two *pesukim*.

¹⁰ And Hashem said, "You had pity on the *kikayon* plant which you did not work for, which you did not make grow. It grew overnight, and was destroyed overnight.

י וַיֹּ֣אמֶר יְהֹוָ֗ה אַתָּ֤ה חַ֙סְתָּ֙ עַל־הַקִּ֣יקָי֔וֹן אֲשֶׁ֛ר לֹא־עָמַ֥לְתָּ בּ֖וֹ וְלֹ֣א גִדַּלְתּ֑וֹ שֶׁבִּן־לַ֥יְלָה הָיָ֖ה וּבִן־לַ֥יְלָה אָבָֽד:

> **A Closer Look**
> Hashem was showing Yonah that he, Yonah, was upset about the *kikayon* plant, even though he had done nothing to make it grow.

¹¹ "So should I not take pity upon Nineveh, the great city, that has more than 120,000 people living there, who do not know their right hands from their left — and also many animals?"

יא וַאֲנִי לֹא אָחוּס עַל־נִינְוֵה הָעִיר הַגְּדוֹלָה אֲשֶׁר יֶשׁ־בָּהּ הַרְבֵּה מִשְׁתֵּים־עֶשְׂרֵה רִבּוֹ אָדָם אֲשֶׁר לֹא־יָדַע בֵּין־יְמִינוֹ לִשְׂמֹאלוֹ וּבְהֵמָה רַבָּה:

A Closer Look
Hashem explains that it was He Who created the people of Nineveh. They are important to Him — even if we do not understand why He needs them. The *kikayon* plant was only one day old, but the great city of Nineveh had been there for a long time. Should He not take much more pity on all those people than Yonah took on the *kikayon* plant?

Did You Know??
The *Book of Yonah* ends here without Yonah answering Hashem. But *Yalkut Shimoni* does tell us what Yonah said:
Yonah fell on his face and said, "Indeed, Hashem, judge the world with mercy!"
Yonah finally understood what true mercy was, and how Hashem wants to be kind to all His creations.

A Closer Look
"People do not know their right hands from their left" means that people do not understand the difference between good and evil.

After we finish reading the *Maftir* from the *Book of Yonah* on Yom Kippur, the Reader reads these three *pesukim* from the *Book of Michah*, Chapter 7.

יח מִי־אֵל כָּמוֹךָ נֹשֵׂא עָוֹן וְעֹבֵר עַל־פֶּשַׁע לִשְׁאֵרִית נַחֲלָתוֹ לֹא־הֶחֱזִיק לָעַד אַפּוֹ כִּי־חָפֵץ חֶסֶד הוּא: יט יָשׁוּב יְרַחֲמֵנוּ יִכְבֹּשׁ עֲוֹנֹתֵינוּ וְתַשְׁלִיךְ בִּמְצֻלוֹת יָם כָּל־חַטֹּאותָם: כ תִּתֵּן אֱמֶת לְיַעֲקֹב חֶסֶד לְאַבְרָהָם אֲשֶׁר־נִשְׁבַּעְתָּ לַאֲבֹתֵינוּ מִימֵי קֶדֶם:

[18] Who is a God like You, Who forgives sins, and forgives the evil doings of His people? He does not stay angry forever, because He wants to be merciful.

[19] He will again have compassion for us, He will forgive our sins, and will throw all His people's sins into the ocean.

[20] May you show only truth to Yaakov, love to Avraham, just as You have sworn to our fathers in the ancient days of old.

Did You Know??

It is easy to see why the *Book of Yonah* is recited on Yom Kippur. It is a book that teaches us about *teshuvah* (repentence). We see that Hashem will forgive even the greatest sinners if they truly repent. Yom Kippur is our special day to repent and beg Hashem to forgive our sins.

That is also why these three *pesukim* are added here, at the end of *Yonah*. They are like Yonah's final statement to Hashem that was mentioned just above. This shows how merciful and forgiving Hashem is.